FREEDOM *on the* MENU

THE GREENSBORO SIT-INS

by CAROLE BOSTON WEATHERFORD

paintings by JEROME LAGARRIGUE

PUFFIN BOOKS

To the courageous students who stood up by sitting down, so we could all have a place at the table —CBW

I would like to thank my entire family, my friends, and the Cormier family for their kindness —JL

PUFFIN BOOKS
Published by the Penguin Group
Penguin Young Readers Group, 345 Hudson Street, New York, New York 10014, U.S.A.
Penguin Group (Canada), 90 Eglinton Avenue East, Suite 700, Toronto, Ontario, Canada M4P 2Y3
(a division of Pearson Penguin Canada Inc.)
Penguin Books Ltd, 80 Strand, London WC2R 0RL, England
Penguin Ireland, 25 St Stephen's Green, Dublin 2, Ireland (a division of Penguin Books Ltd)
Penguin Group (Australia), 250 Camberwell Road, Camberwell, Victoria 3124, Australia
(a division of Pearson Australia Group Pty Ltd)
Penguin Books India Pvt Ltd, 11 Community Centre, Panchsheel Park, New Delhi - 110 017, India
Penguin Group (NZ), 67 Apollo Drive, Rosedale, North Shore 0745, Auckland, New Zealand
(a division of Pearson New Zealand Ltd.)
Penguin Books (South Africa) (Pty) Ltd, 24 Sturdee Avenue, Rosebank, Johannesburg 2196, South Africa

Registered Offices: Penguin Books Ltd, 80 Strand, London WC2R 0RL, England

First published in the United States of America by Dial Books for Young Readers,
a division of Penguin Young Readers Group, 2005
Published by Puffin Books, a division of Penguin Young Readers Group, 2007

1 3 5 7 9 10 8 6 4 2

THE LIBRARY OF CONGRESS HAS CATALOGED THE DIAL EDITION AS FOLLOWS:
Weatherford, Carole Boston, date.
Freedom on the menu : the Greensboro sit-ins / by Carole Boston Weatherford ; illustrations by Jerome Lagarrigue.
p. cm.
Summary: A portrait of the 1960 civil rights sit-ins at the Woolworth's lunch counter in
Greensboro, North Carolina, as seen through the eyes of a young Southern black girl.
ISBN: 0-8037-2860-3 (hardcover)
1. African Americans—North Carolina—Greensboro—Juvenile fiction.
[1. African Americans—North Carolina—Greensboro—Fiction. 2. Civil rights demonstrations—Fiction.
3. Greensboro (N.C.)—Race relations—Fiction.] I. Lagarrigue, Jerome, ill. II. Title.
PZ7.W3535 Fr 2005
[Fic]—dc21 2002013226

Puffin Books ISBN 978-0-14-240894-0

Manufactured in China

Designed by Teresa Kietlinski
Text set in Bembo

Just about every week, Mama and I went shopping downtown. I loved having her all to myself for the afternoon. Whenever it was hot or we got tired, we'd head over to the snack bar in the five-and-dime store. We'd stand as we sipped our Cokes because we weren't allowed to sit at the lunch counter.

Once, I watched a girl swivel a stool as she spooned a banana split. In the empty seat beside her was a purse almost exactly like mine.

"Can I have a banana split?" I begged Mama.

"Not here, Connie," said Mama. "I'll fix you one at home."

"Won't be the same," I grumbled.

All over town, signs told Mama and me where we could and couldn't go. Signs on water fountains, swimming pools, movie theaters, even bathrooms.

WATER
WHITE

Everybody I knew obeyed the signs—except my great-aunt Gertie from New York. Once, when she visited us, she drank from a whites-only fountain and said real loud, "I've never heard of colored water. Have you, Connie?" Then she lifted me up so I could take a sip.

I looked up from the fountain. "Y'all know better than that!" a man scolded.

I started to say "Sorry, mister," but Aunt Gertie just huffed, "I'm too old for silly rules."

It was a real hot day, but the man walked away without taking a drink.

There weren't any signs up in the five-and-dime, but we still knew how it was. Most people didn't expect change anytime soon. But my daddy thought different.

"Dr. King's coming to town," he told us one morning.

"Who's sick?" I asked.

"He's not that kind of doctor, Connie," Daddy laughed. "He's a minister who's working to make things better for us," said Daddy.

"So we can go anywhere we please," said Mama.

"Like the lunch counter?" I asked.

"Yep," said Daddy, "and other places, too."

Later that week, our whole family went to hear Dr. King preach at the college chapel. I didn't really understand all of his speech, but I liked his booming voice. It sounded as if he believed God was on our side. Every few minutes, Mama said, "Amen," and when Dr. King sat down, everyone stood and clapped for a long time.

65¢

An old white lady came up to the boys. "I'm so proud of you," she said clear as a bell so everyone could hear. "I wish someone had done this sooner."

The waitress kept wiping and re-wiping the counter and refilling salt and pepper shakers, sugar pourers, and napkin holders.

Suddenly, the manager came back with a tall policeman.

"Let's go, Connie," said Mama. The manager shooed us right out of the store and then put a Closed sign in the window.

I couldn't wait to tell Brother.

“Why’d your friends do that?” I asked.

“If we can spend money at a store,” said Brother, “it’s only fair that we should be able to eat at the store’s lunch counter.”

“I guess so,” I said. “Think it’ll work?”

“Sometimes it’s important just to try,” said Daddy, rubbing his chin.

The next day, Daddy showed me the newspaper. The headline said: *Negro Students Stand Up By Sitting Down.*

“They sat four hours,” said Daddy, peering over the newspaper.

“I’d be too hungry to wait that long,” I said.

“Connie, they didn’t really want food,” said Daddy. “They wanted to be allowed to get it, same as if they were white. To be treated fairly.”

EQUAL
RIGHTS

By Friday, we heard on the news how hundreds more had joined the sit-ins. "The protests are growing!" I told Daddy.

"I'm joining the sit-ins," Brother said, bursting into the room.

"And I'm going to picket downtown," said Sister. "Tomorrow."

"I want to go, too," I said. "I'm plenty big enough to hold a sign, and I know I can sit."

"It's good that you want to help," said Daddy. "But, Connie, you're still too young for these things."

"I never get to do anything important." I pouted.

"You can help us make picket signs," said Sister. "That's very important."

The next morning, I handed Sister my little flag for her to carry.

"We'll tell you everything when we get home," Brother promised.

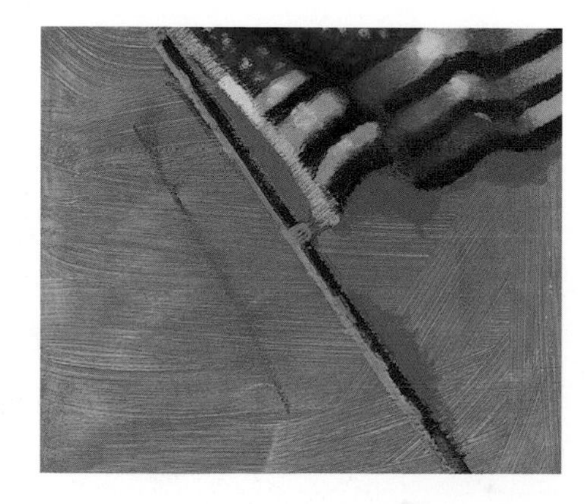

Turns out, I saw the protests on TV. Hundreds of people walked up and down the sidewalks in front of stores, restaurants, and movie theaters. I saw my own sister carrying a picket sign. And there was the back of Brother's head at the lunch counter. My own brother!

"I'm just so proud of them," said Daddy.

"Me, too," I said.

"I just pray there's no trouble," Mama fretted.

After a while, I watched the news on TV almost as much as Mama and Daddy. One night I saw a report on the sit-ins. "That doesn't look like downtown," I said.

"Connie, the sit-ins have spread all over the South," said Daddy.

Just then, the phone rang. I answered it. "Daddy! It's Sister. She got arrested at the lunch counter. She's in jail!"

Sister, who always got A's in school, who hardly ever got in trouble, who was what Mama called "mule-stubborn."

Daddy raced to the police station, but Sister wouldn't *let him* get her out of jail. He told me how the students kept chanting, "Jail not bail! Jail not bail!"

"We can't just leave Sister here with the bad guys," I pleaded.

"She's made up her mind, Connie," said Mama, wiping a tear. "She wants to stay with the other students."

In a few days, Sister came home. "Promise me you'll stop picketing," I begged.

"I can't do that," she said, hugging me tight.

Now, instead of shopping downtown, we had to order from the Sears catalog. Mama and I leafed through the big, thick catalog together, and she even let me help pick things out, but we both knew it wasn't the same. "How long before the sit-ins are over, Mama?" I asked.

"Till folks get what they want," said Mama.

That summer, Mama, Daddy, and I finally went downtown. When we passed Woolworth's, I heard someone shout, "They're serving them!" Daddy stopped so fast that the brakes screeched and Mama and I jolted forward. We parked and ran to the lunch counter.

COFFEE

There sat the women who worked in the restaurant's kitchen. They were all dressed up fancy and eating egg salad!

I can't even stand the smell of egg salad, but I stood and watched them eat every bite. "Looks pretty good," I said. Daddy and I shared big grins.

The next day, Brother, Sister, and I made a special trip downtown. Brother wore a suit and tie. We girls wore hats and white gloves. At the lunch counter, I climbed up on a stool next to them. "We'll have three hot dogs, three French fries, two coffees, one Coke, and one banana split, please," I told that blond-haired waitress.

Sister and Brother sipped coffee and I twisted on my stool while we waited for our meals. Our food soon arrived. As I ate, the waitress plopped an extra cherry on a mound of whipped cream. She still looked nervous, but she smiled at me.

It was the best banana split I ever had.

Author's Note

ON FEBRUARY 1, 1960, four students from North Carolina Agricultural and Technical College sat down at Woolworth's lunch counter in Greensboro, North Carolina, and asked to be served. The college freshmen, seventeen- and eighteen-year-olds—Franklin McCain, David Richmond, Joseph McNeil, and Ezell Blair (now known as Jibreel Khazan)—became known as the Greensboro Four.

"We were kids ourselves," said Joseph McNeil. "After living that lifestyle, of second-class everything, we said, 'Enough is enough.'"

"We didn't like not having dignity and respect," said Franklin McCain. "I went out of that store feeling powerful."

Within days, students from Bennett College, a black, all-girls school, began sitting at the lunch counter, too. White students from other local schools—Woman's College, Greensboro College, and Guilford College—also participated. Students not only sat at lunch counters but made their own signs and marched on downtown sidewalks, urging people not to shop at stores whose lunch counters would not allow blacks to sit down and eat. Often, white hecklers tried to scare off the protesters by calling them names and threatening violence. Some students were arrested, but the Greensboro sit-ins lasted off and on for seven months. High school students carried on the protests after the college students went home for summer break. Student-led sit-ins soon spread throughout the South.

On July 25, 1960, blacks were finally allowed to eat at the Woolworth's lunch counter. The first served were the lunch counter's black workers: Geneva Tisdale, Anetha Jones, Susie Morrison, and Charles Best. "I am very proud of that," said Geneva Tisdale, who worked behind the counter for thirty-five years. "We've come a long way."

After the 1960s sit-ins, students and other supporters successfully challenged segregation in other public places: parks, swimming pools, beaches, theaters, restaurants, libraries, courtrooms, and elsewhere. Since then, sit-ins and other forms of civil disobedience have been used by activists around the world. Environmentalists have "hugged" trees in forests to stop logging operations. Groups have pitched "tent cities," large encampments in urban areas, to protest poverty and homelessness. And international protesters have formed human chains, people standing hand in hand for miles, to focus on social, economic, and political injustices. Like the student sit-ins of 1960, these peaceful forms of resistance send a strong message: Till justice is done, we shall not be moved.

Two of the Greensboro Four, (left to right) Joseph McNeil and Franklin McCain, are joined by Billy Smith and Clarence Henderson in a sit-in protest at the Woolworth lunch counter.